WELCOME TO
PASSPORT TO READING
A beginning reader's ticket to a brand-new world!

Every book in this program is designed to build read-along and read-alone skills, level by level, through engaging and enriching stories. As the reader turns each page, he or she will become more confident with new vocabulary, sight words, and comprehension.

These PASSPORT TO READING levels will help you choose the perfect book for every reader.

READING TOGETHER
Read short words in simple sentence structures together to begin a reader's journey.

READING OUT LOUD
Encourage developing readers to sound out words in more complex stories with simple vocabulary.

READING INDEPENDENTLY
Newly independent readers gain confidence reading more complex sentences with higher word counts.

READY TO READ MORE
Readers prepare for chapter books with fewer illustrations and longer paragraphs.

This book features sight words from the educator-supported Dolch Sight Words List. This encourages the reader to recognize commonly used vocabulary words, increasing reading speed and fluency.

For more information, please visit lbyr.com/passporttoreading.

Enjoy the journey!

Little, Brown and Company
Hachette Book Group
1290 Avenue of the Americas, New York, NY 10104
Visit us at LBYR.com

First Edition: October 2020

Little, Brown and Company is a division of Hachette Book Group, Inc.
The Little, Brown name and logo are trademarks of Hachette Book Group, Inc.

The publisher is not responsible for websites
(or their content) that are not owned by the publisher.

Library of Congress Control Number: 2020937130

ISBNs: 978-0-316-42926-9 (pbk.), 978-0-316-42923-8 (ebook),
978-0-316-42925-2 (ebook), 978-0-316-42924-5 (ebook)

Printed in the United States of America

CW

10 9 8 7 6 5 4 3 2 1

Passport to Reading titles are leveled by independent reviewers applying the standards
developed by Irene Fountas and Gay Su Pinnell in *Matching Books to Readers: Using
Leveled Books in Guided Reading*, Heinemann, 1999.

Christmas Rescue!

Adapted by Elle Stephens

L B

LITTLE, BROWN AND COMPANY
New York Boston

Attention, Miraculous fans!
Look for these words
when you read this book.
Can you spot them all?

snow globe

catfish

sleigh

robot

Marinette is babysitting
her friend Nino's little brother.
His name is Chris.
He shows Marinette his snow globe.

Chris sees a pink chest.

It is full of Christmas presents.

He wants to open his presents now.

But it is not Christmas!

Marinette says
Santa Claus only gives early presents
to very, very good kids.
Chris is not happy to hear this.

Later that day,
it starts snowing.
Marinette and Tikki go outside.

Something strange is happening.

Catfish toys fly through the air.

Toy soldiers march
in the street.

A giant T. rex toy roars!
The toys are looking
for Santa Claus.

"Tikki, spots on!"
Marinette yells.
She turns into
the superhero Ladybug!

Ladybug finds
Santa's sleigh.
It has crashed!
Where is Santa Claus?

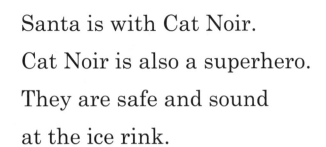

Santa is with Cat Noir.

Cat Noir is also a superhero.

They are safe and sound

at the ice rink.

Ladybug finds them.
But so does the toy army!

A supervillain named
Chris Master has sent the toys.
He wants his
Christmas present early.

Santa Claus says no.

Only very, very good kids get

early presents.

The toys attack!

Ladybug and Cat Noir
help Santa escape.
Ladybug knows how
to find Chris Master.

Ladybug asks Santa Claus
if she can have her
Christmas present early.
Santa says yes.
She is a very, very good kid!

Ladybug has a plan.
She asks for
the same present
as the one Chris Master wants.

Ladybug holds up
her present.
"Come and get it!"
she tells Chris Master.

A helicopter picks up the present,
just as she planned.
Ladybug follows the helicopter.
It leads her to Chris Master.

Chris Master is Nino's little brother!
The evil supervillain Hawk Moth
sent an akuma to his snow globe.
The akumas are butterflies that turn
people into supervillains!

Chris Master sees the superheroes.

His toys capture Cat Noir!

Ladybug saves him.

Chris Master is mad.

Chris Master uses the power
in his snow globe.
It turns the present
into a giant robot!
The huge robot attacks.

Ladybug and Cat Noir fight back.
Cat Noir is ready
to destroy the robot.

But Chris Master does not
want his robot to be destroyed.
He gives his snow globe to Ladybug.
The fight is over.

Ladybug breaks the
snow globe's spell.
She stops Hawk Moth!

Santa Claus thanks
Ladybug and Cat Noir.
Santa goes back
to the North Pole.

Chris Master turns back
into a boy.
His toy army turns back
into regular toys.

Chris Master is gone.

Now Marinette and Chris
are excited to wait for Christmas!